"Considering how much I love Richard Chiem's writing, and given how its uncanny snare and sweep of life's especially agile, prompt, messed, lithe, sharp, and heartbreaking things leaves me stiffed of summarizing words, I think I'll just nominate his work for immortality."

— Dennis Cooper, author of *The Marbled Swarm* and the *George Miles Cycle*

YOU PRIVATE PERSON

RICHARD CHIEM

MMXXIV

for Frances

Previously published by Sorry House Press
First edition 2012 from Scrambler Books

www.withanxbooks.com
Cover Design by Tori Huynh
Layout by Jon Nix
WAX010
ISBN 979-8-9874787-7-6

CONTENTS

"The first fiction is your name."
-Eileen Myles

FORWARD

It's easier and easier to find evidence of mass hysteria in one's day to day life in the year 2024. The world as it is now is one I hardly recognize when I remember the world in which I first read You Private Person and the world in which I subsequently first met its author, Richard Chiem. I mention mass hysteria for a reason. When Richard asked me to write this foreward, I Googled "how to write a foreward for a book." Then I took my battered copy of You Private Person to the park with a jug of pink lemonade and a beach towel and read it cover to cover in one sitting, surrounded by the smells (grilling) and sounds (merriment) of a child's 8th birthday party. When I looked away from the page to think, I noticed that staring at the cloudless blue sky felt no different than continuing to read. Richard and his book are alike. I wish all people were like Richard, and I wish all people were like Richard's characters. To know Richard and to read Richard is to feel twin emotions; known, but not exposed; embraced, but not suffocated.

— Rachel Bell, June 2024
author of *Loving the Ocean*
Won't Keep It From Killing You

sociopaths

animals with expression

I smoke a cigarette, imagine flocks of birds in the blue sky, and realize I am always going to be a sad person. Birds are so fun to imagine. This all comes from years of wanting to know how to fly standing out on balconies pretending sex is the same as flight because surely geese can feel glowing in the air like I do when bedrooms soften after foreplay, when language barely works, much like animal speech. Only by repeating each other's names. I do believe all birds are named Chirp.

I whisper my thoughts of wanting to make her feel like how geese might feel, shaping the words quietly in her ear. Shadows on the walls slowly circle around the comfortable bed as though lowering the temperature in the room a few untraceable degrees. Something is very full in the way we lay together. Out in the hallway there is a telephone ringing she tells me we should definitely ignore.

She straddles me and wants me to stop smoking. She can smell cigarettes on me.

I call her Geese for no reason.

Feeling insignificant, watching traffic from a balcony in a poor house, we don't move a muscle all afternoon. Lights turn on slowly. I notice how comfortable we are in our underwear before work.

Outside cars glimmer down black highways, all empty

seemingly in a row.

Mass transit washes over me. I am only as fast as her face moving into expression. Everything else is background noise, muffled and out of focus.

She stares at the motion light inside the bus and says, What a shitty day. The bus hisses and Mary has to be at work for her housekeeping job in about twenty minutes. She's worried she's going to be late and then terminated. Sunlight can make her feel unattractive when she's thinking about more time so I have my hand at her thigh where I calm her through small squeezes, small reminders that she's the shit.

Behind her ear I am communicating to her lobes, You are the employee of the month.

She calls me a strange bird.

I say, Geese. Have a good day at work.

living room

On the balcony there is a good twenty minutes she feels like she wasn't thinking about anything at all but how fast the cars are moving and what to eat for dinner later. The sky appears to be thinking about clouds but does not quite produce them and there is some gray that gathers and she ignores it. Richard watches blue smoke rise from his cigarette in the ashtray and leaves, saying, I have to go to the bathroom real quick. She says okay and watches a man on the street stumble home while crossing a red light. A yellow car nearly hits him and then goes honking off in the distance.

An ambulance is screaming en route and Mary follows along with her eyes and takes a moment to feel corrupt inside and does not take a breath. She is so still and focused it's as though her eyes are changing colors and circulating. She barely notices that she's biting her lip. She imagines a paramedic pumping his palms into a chest trying to resuscitate someone unconscious because too much time has already passed. She imagines there is nothing left to be done while the ambulance disappears from sight.

Mary turns around to the kitchen and wonders if the chicken has finished simmering.

She wonders if she should tell Richard about the

ambulance and her train of thought but decides not to. Something is burning.

Her buttocks march underneath her cotton panties in a gentle, unbreakable code back to the kitchen. The air conditioning is humming cold air through the vents. After a few pokes from a fork she judges that the meat is still good to eat. Richard brings her a pepper shaker and thinks, I am definitely an ass man.

He says, There is something on the back of your neck. He kisses her there.

She says, Wow, and she wonders what she really means. Sometimes she cannot tell whether or not she is being cruel or sarcastic or playful on purpose, especially when she doesn't have anything clever to say. Inside her head, intentions misfire. Her movements are pale around Richard. She ponders and looks at him silently. She feels annoyed by his passive face and smells burnt chicken when he places his hands on her stomach.

Chicken and rice and green beans.

Red wine and burning candle wax sit on top of the white linen lace on the table.

He says, I thought we were vegetarian.

I don't know, she says. I'm feeling weird.

She does seem quite transported. Her voice holds a weak yet affectionate tone and her stomach is cold beneath his hands. There is something obviously wrong and he immediately wants to know, moving closer but cautiously.

What happened?

I'm not sure, she says. But I feel angry.

Why angry? Angry at what?

Do you remember the man I told you about one

time? When I was younger?

Wait, Richard says. The man that touched you? Yeah, she says without levity, without much.

Yes, says her voice.

I think I saw him today at work.

on a normal day

No one talks in the family and it's absolute madness around here all the time, her mother says. Much too quiet for a kid growing up, especially for a girl like her, always upside down somewhere on a couch or hanging from a tree. Seven people living in the house all the time and no one had a damn thing to say to anyone else unless it was to get out of the way or to borrow some money or to kick and scream recklessly because it was too hot outside.

Maybe she is trying to break some long-going bad tra dition by moving away so far from her mother. Generations of sad people breeding sadder people. Maybe that's why my baby doesn't pick up that pen anymore.

Maybe that's why she doesn't write her mother. I remember that my girl never wanted to be a princess. Dresses were the devil. Shoes constrained her until she grew red to tears. She managed a face so pink you could have sworn I had a knife on me. She was so frightened I would let her run off sometimes for days to find solitude. She preferred birds, climbing trees, and eating strange fruit. Falling from various points of the tall oak tree in our back yard I remember her marking her progress down in her spiral green notebook. She would measure how high she fell. She survived and remembered every fall from the tall oak tree and came home to tell me about what it felt like to be alone.

Mary said she could survive anything. She told me every day.

Late autumn one year, I remember being a very cruel mother. I remember telling her, Green eyes are a recessive gene, Mary darling. You are going to have to stare at people twice as hard and twice as long for them to really see you. I think I stopped being her mother there. Right then.

She was always such a good listener. She knew what grudges were right away.

Her eyes developed this seductive color when she made eye contact. Any man, it doesn't matter who, she could make him feel greater and indispensable like he is the sun she revolves around like he's superman. But she doesn't love you. I am telling you she is dangerous because she doesn't love you. Her eyes carry a false affinity and everyone is fooled. She doesn't know what she's doing with you.

She won't be able to love you back, Richard. Because no one really sees her. Not my angel, her mother says. Not my Mary.

Richard breathes into the receiver of the phone, staring at Mary while he does. It's already early in the morning sometime around six and Mary is getting dressed and get-ting ready for work. She is a balancing act of coffee, keys, her jacket and many small bags. Her mother calls every morning. She is so clockwork it has stopped feeling so disturbing.

But I am superman, Richard whispers into the phone.

Mary kisses Richard on the cheek and rushes out the door to catch a bus and he opens the blinds in the window and watcher her jaunt away.

You never protected her, Richard says to Mary's mother. Please don't call back.

So do you think you can? Do you think that's what she wants protection? Richard?

classically trained

Outside a cafe Richard is listening closely to his friend Thom talk about personal problems. He briefly becomes distracted by the skyline. Black birds are making V's in the distance. Richard begins to get concerned that something out of his control is happening. He feels a strange shift. The weather is nice, but it's hard to stay calm.

A man dies today, Thom says.

Thom looks off vacantly at clouds as though he doesn't care what it is to see out there. Thom seems burdened by old memories but pretends today everything is fine. A breeze does not move them. They do not register the cold. The two friends remain still and unnerved. The sky is courting the earth with darkening blue and strange clouds and Richard plays the table with his fingers and forgets the name for 'cilantro' and picks up the cilantro a little bewildered and feels strangely blank. Richard stares at Thom blowing perfect circle smoke rings in the air. Richard questions what he has in his hands: a pale green thing. What is this called, he is thinking, what the hell?

Cilantro, says Richard's voice.

A man dies today, Thom says.

There are a group of officers around this John's body, Thom says, and his eyes are open because he died very comfortably resting at home. His feet are up against this red expensive ottoman. Television's off and there's an open book on the coffee table. He watches the shadows on the wall and how the ceiling never moves. The kitchen is filthy because a few scattered beer bottles here and there never killed anyone, right? The man calls the bottles dead sol-diers and he drinks them bottle after bottle until they're empty and leaves them on the counter without thinking about the future at all. He had no future. He was zen. Officers arrive and write things down in their notepads. The man just lays there dead and buzzing and grinning his last beaming expression. Lieutenant Chloe arrives to the scene of the crime looks down and thinks the John looks happy. Looked happy. There is a hole three inches deep in his head and the wound resembles apple pie.

The autopsy: he died due to heavy trauma to his head. Three particular objects are lodged inside the hole at the center of his head like candles on a cake and there are no exit wounds. It's as if the John wanted to keep them there for his own personal reason. Unfortunately the detectives working the investigation worry about paperwork and barely realize the spectacle of what happened to the John. Which is a moment of true art. The first object found in his head is a small pocket knife.

The knife was thrown from an incredible distance maybe twenty or thirty feet away and thrown by a young boy who has never kissed anyone before. The young boy four days later is courageous enough to ask out the first love of his life, calling his own shot.

The second object is a heavy bullet. It was shot by a woman who cannot speak English but she wants to learn

English. She makes all her meals at home, falling in love with her neighbor across the hall. She keeps a gun that she fires into the wall when she can't take being alone inside anymore.

The third object is a note folded eight times. Blood makes the words illegible.

Everyone is slightly baffled.

Looking down again at the Dead John after the autopsy Lieutenant Chloe changes her mind and contemplates things. She is getting exact. Her colleagues notice her deep thinking. The room has a nice stillness hovering around them and the doctors are puzzled reading X ray scans. She decides and says out loud, He looks like he's in love. It goes on forever.

Thom ends his monologue and sips coffee.

Richard is looking at Thom without blinking and fights off a smile.

After listening it's as though Richard is waking from a stupor. In the glass window he has never seen tinier pupils in his eyeballs.

Richard asks, What is wrong with you?

Thom says, I feel pretty zen today.

Thom punches himself in the head twice and says, Violence.

* * * *

Classically trained as a pianist since he was a child, Thom measures beats in the silence between them with no wind, no breeze. The feeling of knowing changes into comfort. He can hear a mathematical quiet. He decides today that he is alive and he says, I am alive. Richard takes a slow drag from a new cigarette and exhales. They both feel a deep reservoir of peace in the everyday routine of things. People here talk about bad parking and the weather every day. They are sitting at a wicker table outside a cafe they always go to where there is a Time Crisis II machine. Near them a young server is waiting to pick up an order and her eyes follow drowsily as people continue to pass outside everyone walking in the same direction like a slow monot-onous parade. Richard imagines undressing Mary secretly in his head before pondering the people inside the cafe again. They move in self-contained worlds and unbreachable swarms. He wonders how he can make them all stop what they are doing.

He wipes his face with the back of his hand and smells his coffee from the ceramic cup and looks across the way to the other sidewalk.

Balls of pigeons take flight across the street and reassemble on the ledge of a brick building and they do this a few times. Thom says, The sky looks like turtle shells.

Richard thinks, We all talk about the sky too much. But it's always there I guess, he thinks quietly in his inner monologue and takes comfort in that.

Inside the cafe, there is a posh looking couple dressed in matching black and silver and they are having fish with the head still attached. The man is getting his food everywhere on the table. He is not really a chewer. The woman seems to be having a conversation to herself, since they are not making eye contact with each other. They do not look up or acknowledge their servers.

Thom says, They seem like terrible people.

Just then the woman inside makes a face staring at Thom and his smoke rings. She even points at Thom and Richard even though they are only a few inches away on the other side of the glass. She points and keeps pointing until the man she is with makes the same grimace. Bits of food can be seen stuck in their gums and teeth. Thom's expression falls apart in a second. Richard thinks again about how very thin the layer of glass between them is. The glass is very thin.

Thom smiles at the couple with slowness. He pretends he is a clown with one constant happy expression. For a few minutes his face does not change expression and the couple deepens in their seats, turning their faces away. They chew food uncomfortably.

Thom imagines his face unchanged for years.

Although they try to keep having dinner, sometimes they turn back to the window and Thom is still there smiling from ear to ear. He is good at not blinking.

So what does Mary do? Thom asks.

She's an inventor.

Oh yeah? What did she invent?

Everything, Richard says. I think she invented everything. But no one gives her credit.

Richard pauses and stares at the couple inside.

She's a housekeeper for now, Richard says. Working for some hotel downtown.

*　*　*　*

The couple inside the cafe has asked the hostess to

come over to complain about Thom. Thom is still there smiling. The hostess seems to be touched by what Thom is doing or understands and replies back to the couple with short and apologetic moves from her shoulders as if saying, *There is nothing we can do, sir.*

Thom asks without changing his face, What are we doing here? Why the meet up?

Mary, says Richard's voice.

There's a man Mary remembers from her past that she has seen staying at the hotel. And I think this is the same guy that molested her when she was younger.

You're kidding, Thom says.

Richard says nothing. His mind is creating a vast discipline.

Thom says, Richard, you're scaring me.

Before departing the cafe and leaving a generous tip Thom makes his fingers into the shape of a pistol and gestures at the couple inside with a quick twitch of his wrist and he tells them, You're dead. You're dead.

Richard looks around the ceilings and the walls of the restaurant for a no smoking sign but finds none.

I am scaring myself, Richard says.

Let's go make a mistake, Richard says.

act natural

She can see her face go bright in the window when a cloud moves above the hotel. It fills a sweet agony in her eyes and she almost admires the painful feeling when she goes back to work. She feels so relaxed it's as though she could be asleep walking through the dimly lit hallways.

Mary sighs and says, I hate work, I hate work, walking through the luxury suite on the balls of her heels completely unaware what day of the week it is. In every room behind every closed door everyone seems to be sleeping still. Mary feels today is maybe Tuesday.

There are towels piled in her arms and her hair is up tightly wound in a knot when she passes by the paintings along the walls.

If Mary listens very closely and she often does there is music playing above her from hidden speakers from the intercom system of the luxurious hotel.

Elevator music accompanies her pacing back and forth and up and down the hallways. Green carpet and simple diamond patterns line the floors.

Sometimes she stares at the clock and wonders what Richard is doing. While waiting for the heavy clothes to dry in the gigantic machines while waiting for the dumbwaiter full of dirty laundry to arrive Mary slows herself down and takes a breath. She squints her eyes at custom-ers as though they are made of light. They give her tips and pocket change even when she does not ask for tips or pocket change. All she wants is to be left alone to her duties. She folds towels and towels with intrigue, feeling high and happy in a corner somewhere far away from view.

Inside a mop closet next to the cleaning supplies, she hides and takes a small drag from a joint she rolled for herself this morning. The drug moves a calm haze in her and she feels like an empty vessel moving from room to room from task to task until it's time for her to clock out and leave for home. She feels no emotion, she thinks, walking wide eyed again through the hallways avoiding eye contact and talking to people. She is surviving socially again. She is a slave to the all details that she is suddenly taking all in.

She remembers telling Richard in bed what the drugs mean to her.

The high gives her a private room in public spaces.

She has about forty-five minutes left until her shift is over.

Richard replies, Every day we are hustling.

She enjoys catching a view of any clocks, any watch face, something she likes to do at work to pass the time to calm herself down because she tends to get anxious. Long hours make her anxious. She's counting down the minutes before she sees him again.

She says, Richard is so fun to miss. More people pass her in the lobby, maybe a few dozen but no one bothers her. She receives five dollars when she cleans up a client's dinner and notices his untouched steamed vegetables.

Something like Mozart plays again from the speakers.

People pass on in crowds rushing parallel on either side of her.

Commotion stirs throughout the hotel and the guests are rapidly leaving their rooms suggesting a spectacle happening outside. There is an eerie kind of murmur. Every-one is heading one direction toward the exits. There are many people with their hands over their mouths near the windows. She is brushing by coworkers on her way out-side. One says I have to close the registers tonight I wonder what's happening outside.

She leaves and says, I will let you know.

Mary interprets panic on every face and this makes her feel sober.

She has two hands and ten fingers. She is awake. She follows the crowd to another crowd outside the grand lobby of the hotel and there are two police cars, an ambulance and a fire engine. The siren lights are rotating but there is no sound.

Someone jumped from the rooftop, some older man, Mary learns.

They think it might be suicide, she learns.

She meets a family on the outskirts of the large crowd. They seem more excited than afraid and they tell Mary everything they've heard very engagingly. The father holds his daughter in his arms raising her on his shoulders so she can catch a better glimpse of things.

Without really knowing why Mary asks someone in the crowd for a cigarette and then for a light. It's her first cigarette in months.

The pavement looks wet and shiny. She realizes how many trees are surrounding the hotel and there has to be hundreds.

So someone killed himself.

I have twenty-two minutes left until I get to go home, she says.

That's like one Simpson's episode.

The door takes a while to open but when she manages to get through the threshold she finds Richard reading comfortably on the couch. There is an open bottle of wine next to him and a fresh pack of cigarettes. There are only a few smokes missing from the pack the television is turned on and the living room is spotless. He must have freshened up, she thinks, and she looks around. She tries to be quiet trying to surprise him maybe, tiptoeing closer.

Richard looks up from the words on the page. It is as though he has come back into the room when their eyes meet. Richard smiles wearily and looks at her.

Mary says, Hello. She kisses him on the cheek.

No one but me knows how soft his cheeks are, she thinks.

Richard rises and says, I've made dinner. It's in the kitchen.

Mary says, Oh yeah?

She turns around and is surprised by a whole suckling pig roasted on a metal tray and aluminum foil and the sudden smells of garlic and oils. There is an apple in the pig's mouth and his eyes are baked and look crusty. There seems to be no side dishes to go with the meat and she asks, You made a whole pig?

Richard says nothing.

He seems to be already chewing something looking exhausted and worn out placing his book down on the cushions. Light carries dust through the room and his face registers ecstasy when she makes eye contact again. Instead of winking he does not stop looking at her. He walks backwards into the kitchen to get food for the two of them.

He is performing for her. He is trying to make her laugh. The television screen turns blue on mute. Those eyes he has can maneuver her out of her shell and make her float there in the living room and almost die of laughing. She laughs like crazy at his goofy dancing as he goes back and forth from the kitchen bringing back more and more food. In the light he appears more toned. She enjoys his veins and arms.

She appreciates the light and the clean space of her home. Richard is still dancing and not talking much.

She takes a hit. The weed pulls her mind to the back of her head and she feels slowness. The windows are cool and perfectly see through. Mary exhales as if exhaling is an art form watching her own breath travel to the ceiling and feeling good and stationary. Her eyes feel at home.

She theorizes her size and imagines his. The kitchen dims then glows and she doesn't know what she is really thinking really.

Mary leans her chin on Richard's neck and says, I think that's why your pupils get so big when you're high. Because you're trying to see everything.

She says, I have never seen pupils so tiny.

What, he says. I don't get it. I don't understand.

Shut up, Mary says, and she kisses him. She tries to communicate with her body and lips. The massage from her tongue makes Richard feel as though he is slowly being pulled down towards a lower depth by weights, a dreamy and loving depth.

She guides him towards the nearest piece of furniture: a leather love seat in the center of the living room. Refusing to let go of the kiss and refusing to open their eyes, they move like people blindfolded. Richard bumps his knee against the coffee table and murmurs in pain. Mary fights off a smile before she smiles.

He says, Fuck.

She says, Fuck.

She straddles him over his waist and pushes him down like a domino with her lower thighs. She enjoys these transformations before sex. She thinks, Birds do the same thing when flying without moving their wings.

But, he says, Wait. Hold on.

Richard gently moves out from underneath her and wipes his face. His hands push her shoulders away until he can see her face again. Strangely at this distance they look remarkably ugly to each other.

I have to tell you something, he says.

I did something today, he says.

He says, Thom and I did.

She moves her hair back while her body winds down from a hot peak. She shakes her head. She washes her face with her hands and waits.

She looks around again at the clean house and reinterprets his intentions. She imagines his anxiousness trying to calm itself by doing chores and cooking and waiting for her to get home. Feeling out of her head, Mary waits.

What are you talking about? She asks.

The man that touched you.

I pushed him off a building, Richard says.

maybe sprout wings

Upstairs Mary finishes the bottle of wine Richard left behind and she doesn't know what to do now. Maybe sprout wings. Their last conversation replays in her head in imagined voices. Her eyes glaze and glaze. She can hear the ice tinkling the glass. The roasted pig is getting colder on the table. Mary walks over and takes the apple from the pig's mouth and takes a bite.

When she yells at Richard it is the first time she has raised her voice in front of him.

She says, I don't need protection.

Do you understand?

That was incredibly selfish of you.

She says, Do you understand?

When she yells at him she unhinges. Everything in the body rises and even her teeth cramp. The head becomes a very small, hot room. When he leaves, she aims her voice through the door down the hallway while he stays quiet and says nothing.

In the morning Mary makes coffee but makes too much. She realizes Richard has not come home yet and his phone is off. Why would his phone be off? There is a cool fog and the smell of wet leaves coming from uphill. Her lungs push her ribcage. She watches a stick bug rise from the pile of sticks and stones beyond her feet on the balcony and wonders how long it has been there. What makes it finally come out of hiding? Inside her, there are organs and what she thinks a soul is. She wants to go see the ocean all of a sudden.

the rivalry of dancers

What if they made a movie about us? The first scene has to be in bed when she first wakes up with her new short hair and she feels how cold the room is from her bed sheets, the same room the same bed but everything is colder and more permeable, air is gentle. Right now she wants to teleport in a way similar to tasting sugar how it dissolves on the tongue and goes elsewhere to the body. She has always wanted this intimate ability, slipping through time and space like ripping off clothes on a muggy day.

A naked body in his city.

She just happens to be there. She smells the ocean from her mind. California is in her blood.

She thinks, what do you have room for? Who do you want in that room?

Once I was you, she says to the mirror. She is alone in the Northwest with a million people. Outside, the world is hallowed clean by the morning. She falls asleep often wondering when he will return the emails and she dreams an entire novel in a five-minute nap:

He is the only one among them on stage not dancing. He is standing in the middle where the light blooms on the wood. He is waiting with his hands in his pockets like he's the tallest man for miles around. There is a look of astonishment on his face. He is completely ignoring the dancers. He is a monument.

Strong lean women floating through the air like how snow dreams of the ground.

But I don't give a fuck, he says.

I don't ever give a fuck, she says.

She says, I want to be down there. But I don't want to dance. I don't want to dance at all. I want to stand there with you like a monument.

He is there, he is right there.

When he teleports it's like dial up teleporting. From an airplane, to an airport, to a taxi.

His text message will ask a poem:

(1/2) Are you working? There is a lot you can have by
 wanting. Envisioning
a house where I never lived, you could not convince
 me we'd spent but

(2/2) one life together.

HER: Are you awake? Describe the
house to me.

the first time
or
someone like me would have a chance in a movie

She says, I'm unique by being quiet and withholding. She looks away from her dashboard. She make-believes the apocalypse has already happened while she stares at her hands resting on the steering wheel. She sighs and remembers she can relax the aching tension in her body and imagines things melting: body parts then ice cream.

The sunlight hugs / warms her small figure in the car while she waits there for me, finding a mirror on the back flap thing. Behind her there are no other cars only wide open road. You look really sleepy, she calls out, trying for my attention and waves at me manically in the parking lot, looking so sincere. There is happiness and something else. She is a natural.

She drives sometimes closing her eyes for a long time. Somehow we find ourselves feeling fragile and despondent but together again, carpooling home after work just after sunset, day in and day out. The sky is one gigantic conscious blooming cloud. The reports are saying, There is a super storm coming very soon in CALIFORNIA. There is no wind again when I lick my finger to check to know for myself. There is thunder in the background and people looking up at the lightning.

Our summer place is up on the hillside. The body feels weepy and exhausted along this steep incline. Pebbles shoot up beneath the car and mimic the sound of rain. The NO WAVE pop song on the radio ruins our lives again, she says, and we stay inside the car until the song ends / the song fades to commercials and transitions into another pop song. I like that we wait in the car for songs to end before we get out. She is trying to shrink her stomach and orders her sandwich without chips or a drink. She touches my back pockets in public. She pretends secretly to be a model, she imagines she is a famous underground model, but plans to eat like a pig beast later tonight since we're all very close to death.

She is trying to be small around me unembarrassed in line to pay at the register at the diner. I think this place is a DENNY'S because it looks and smells like a DENNY'S. We look like we have not slept for like three or four days or something, she says as though a camera is there above us, filming everything about us. What if the air was a camera, she asks. She asks, Do you like performance? Do you like performing?

The florescent light makes me feel dirty. She mentions again about being useless, feeling useless, whis-pered in my ear. She says, Let's go be useless some-where. She is looking for but somehow does not see me. She imagines herself already leaving the diner and appears spaced out before she actually leaves the diner. The receipt is printing, the man says at the reg-ister. The man looks up at me from the register. For some reason we can hear NO WAVE pop songs really muffled everywhere we go. We leave for the parking lot. We go back and forth to each other's places for months in the same cars.

The first time a girl makes me pie she picks me up from work she brings me the pie wrapped inside aluminum foil and becomes really shy around me. I remember opening the aluminum foil really slowly like I was unbuttoning her shirt not seductively but carefully because I didn't want her to be shy around me anymore. She leans on a wall. She puts one leg up. She writes episodic screenplays and shows me Los Angeles with small car rides. I help her move from one apartment to the next and undress her if the mood is right / feeling either attractive or abandoned. She films our weekend on her camera and wins all the awards at the smaller film festivals.

She says, I think we're onto something. She reaches for my crotch and makes me feel masculine in the dark. We secretly do not like the same NO WAVE pop songs. She speaks about romance and relationships and tells me she loves me as though quoting a movie.

back pockets full
of dynamite

The dead inside is beautiful. That is what was written on her arm. Chloe went to bed and somehow at some point during the night woke up to write something down on her arm, the dead inside is beautiful, to remember for later. But she doesn't remember ever writing the words down, and her mind draws a blank. She has no recollection or definite feeling. Eventually after a few minutes of waking up and clearing the cobwebs, she starts to admire the phrase, the words on her arm, and tries to imagine why, why would she think that? What dead? She keeps it written on her forearm and clenches her hand when she looks in the mirror and brushes her teeth. The morning is already hot and humid and bright. There is the wonderful feeling she has when she gives up on something and stops caring, in every little breath in her lungs. She says, The dead inside is beautiful. Okay.

She slips on her clothes and looks for her keys. Her blouse is unbuttoned until she gets to the door, looking at herself in the mirror. She has a bagel in her mouth and her hair is tied back. She leaves the radio on but has turned off all the lights, locked all of her doors. Everything she calls and knows as home is all under control, she doesn't have to worry, not looking back as she leaves her apartment for work. She starts walking down the hallway.

When the elevator doors open, there is a naked man inside. He is all naked except he is wearing a ski mask and he is trying to cover himself, crouching inside his arms and hands in the corner. Chloe keeps repeating, Oh my God, and steps backwards against the wall. He runs embarrassed on to her floor, apologizing over and over again before sprinting out of view. Chloe goes inside the elevator and watches her face come together in the reflection of the copper elevator doors, realizing she is in the slightest way shak-ing her head. Because she does not push a button, just for a minute the elevator stays in the half glass half concrete shaft, daylight beginning on the other side of the wall. She says, Okay, okay, and rubs her chest, a little mindless.

the same thing we do every night, Pinky

Transcript from a voice recording

— This guy comes up to me on the street and gives me a dollar. I look up to him and I don't know why he's there and I'm looking at this dollar. It's morning outside and I can hear the city everywhere. Traffic passing, people passing, birds ahead, good air. Usually I'm on the go, I have been assigned to go somewhere and I need to be there pronto. Today I was heading to work when this guy comes up to me and gives me this dollar. So I stopped myself and slowed down. I slowed myself down, missing the green light on my crosswalk. Missing the crosswalk makes me late another five minutes to work. But I look up. The man looks astonished. He watches me peer up from the dollar and opens his mouth. He nearly caresses my face when he reaches out and embraces my shoulder. Something softer for a moment replaces the air, as though lighter air. The man frighteningly enough resembles Bill Murray with a beard, Bill Murray donning a trench coat with another smaller trench coat strapped underneath, the smaller one being a magenta color, like a dark red licorice color trench coat. Nothing about Bill Murray's outfit makes sense to me but he feels familiar and non-threatening. He stands in front of me. His look is very serious and ebbing into the slowness of the atmosphere with his blue eyes, his presence is this gentle wave thing. It's surreal but okay. Bill Murray tells me, No one will ever believe you.

— No one will ever believe you.

— That's what he said to me.

— That's what—Bill Murray. Bill Murray said to me.— Right now I'm driving—right now I'm heading to work and I'm going to flirt with everyone that walks in there. I don't care, won't care. I can talk to strangers for hours. There will be something about me that feels disturbing to someone. I am soft eyes on command. I am a perfect body, a perfect soul. I am working the graveyard shift at CVS until the sun rises. I am going to look at everyone dead set straight in the eyes and pretend I can hear music playing.

Whenever we are talking, I can hear music playing. In our conversations, I will be quietly and gladly transported.

Everyone is the same. I can stare at my wife or a fat man or my best friend or my girlfriend or any complete stranger in the same way as every customer that walks in here. The door alarm rings electronic bells. There is a pretty blonde. There is a drunk man in a business suit. There are teenagers in hoodies gathering near the alcohol. The pretty blonde is taking her time, looking at magazines. There is another man in a trench coat that I thought was going to rob the store. Bill Murray has followed me into the store. Everyone is the same.

— At 2 AM someone came into CVS and tipped me a dollar after buying cigarettes. I think he tipped me a dollar because I looked so miserable. That's what really happened. Everything comes back to a bad day somehow. I looked so terrible and beautiful someone actually tipped me a dollar. I've heard Bill Murray does play pranks on people though. He does pranks all the time. I am not sure what did or did not happen last night. But I have this dollar.

* * * *

Thom makes a three-way call to Richard and Mary and leaves a message. His change in breath suggests he's been smoking again. In the background, occasionally cars pass and once there is a chime from a bicycle. Whenever Thom pauses for breath, there is a sense he is happy, there is a sense he is being more assertive in his speech. Because of the time difference, the time is 3:12 AM Pacific Time when Thom calls from Boston. Both Mary and Richard listen to the message and both wait until the next morning to reply and call back. Cold air unveils the morning and the rooms are blue. The recording is stored in the satellites in the air and in their phones next to their beds while they both feel careless and nearly unconscious.

They are pretending they know Thom is going to be okay. They will ignore his calls. They are never really going to be good with this—Mary and Richard. They are not good with returning phone calls.

If you stand outside and predict lightning, you will be surprised either way right or wrong. Consequences are certain. Everyone knows this. Thom is three hours away all the time. He exists in a separate, almost parallel world, a frame of mind when everyone was getting along and trusting still. Something alive grows passive between friends over the years and does not die, is the common **story.**

Your closest friends are tall trees in a storm. Thom says this waking up sore the next morning, hungover with a headache. He is barely able to recall last night and feels for the dollar in his pocket and searches for his cell phone.

we are a goldmine

If you were wearing a ribbon I would use my teeth to untie the knot for as long as it takes me to untie a knot. I want to steal a car and drive it to you. I want to be closer. There are a thousand miles between me and where I will be soon.

I want a hotel building in the dark just to ourselves so I can have you in one hundred rooms and cook you something large in a large kitchen. In the morning we can run in the hallways in your underwear. We can dance in the hallways in your underwear. We can bite each other in every white jacuzzi,with the steam is going with the lights down. There are towels on the floor and open bottles of champagne. Everywhere we can see, I want to say I can have you there. The music is playing. The ceiling lights behind you have been on forever. On your face you're contemplating never opening your eyes again. On the bed you wonder how light you are. I whisper, I know how to hold you in the air. I know how to make the world a feather.

There are boys around you smoking a cigarette in the forest. In the house behind you there are curtains on fire and girls you've known since grade school lighting their cigarettes. You like the colors red and yellow: something you see in the distance from your house.

I am running and weaving between trees in the forest

chased by wolves and little foxes and already I am feeling impossible to be taken alive. There are men chasing me too with guns and malice. I can hear your voice pressing me to keep going. I know we know I am on my way to see you. The way I ignore branches and shrubbery is careless. I am always later than you want me to be. My face is red with scratches from the sticks and leaves and trees. Running from state line to state line I eat wolves guns and little foxes for breakfast. Behind you the house is burning.

Because I am running in a business suit and tie everyone on the street believes I am part of some strange movie. My dress shoes leave the pavement damaged. They each wonder where I am going. They all wonder how long I will go for. This is how I miss you. Our story for a brief moment occupies the minds of others then the city continues and then slows then goes quiet. They're thinking about us. For years they remember us at random. I run for days in the woods. I want to hold you throughout time. Behind you the house is burning with the people asleep. There is no use in saving them. I am always later than you want me to be. You register me as fast as I register you with your expressive face as I appear from the dark. The leaves vibrate on the trees and the fire burns and burns. You don't turn around even when the house is burning even when I am right behind you.

I want to say, I outran everyone and everything to get here, but realize we are alone. Above your chin, our eyes share a hue. The fire crackles. The trees too.

Did you know people can snap out of depression. Did you know you can have me anywhere like inside your ear.

what if, Wendy

"All these people drinking lover's spit" sings from the small alarm clock radio baby speakers on a low volume on the thin dresser between the two beds like it's the last pop song of the evening's broadcast, like it's the last song ever, and she doesn't say much. She points wordlessly across the room at herself in a wall mirror. She doesn't really move much either. She imagines quietly in her mind what is there in front of her: she is sitting on the floor with someone inches away, a man she met at the bar. She imagines a man who behaves in such a familiar way around her in such a casual setting, she can lose herself in being a pri-vate person, finally a private person.

Feeling rejected on the street when stray dogs ignore her, she cries happy tears when the same song plays on two different radio stations. Sounds seem to lather behind her when she walks throughout the city sometimes, even when she is inside.

The Universe is taking care of her in strange and funny ways. *Lover's Spit* is playing again on both stations.

The carpet is green with diamond patterns and feels stiff as a board beneath her feet. She likes sitting on the floor. She likes leaning on the wall where it meets the floor on her back beneath the yellow metal lamp.

Okay, she says. One, two, three, four.

* * * *

Jesse feels as though he is living on the edge of something like he is going through deeply traumatic times but believes he's still behaving like someone sane and rational. There is something ceremonious in being alone in the city. He watches and admires common strangers and remembers them and keeps them as though they were episodes in his long life, as though his life was a sitcom on television. His good memory keeps getting better and continues to make him a sad person. He knows more beautiful information and goes to the same places. He remembers names and faces.

Sitting closely next to her, he begins to tear his life apart. His phone has no missed calls except from blocked numbers and creditors.

They meet at a bar share a few cigarettes and decide to not exchange names. They gaze back and forth long enough to realize that their goals were a match.

She says, I was hoping we would delude each other. He says, My face has remained unchanged for twenty-nine years. I may have been waiting for this for twenty-nine years.

She doesn't really move much when the song plays again. She lets him talk and vent and she watches him from the bed laying down. She has always wanted to be a destroyer. Jesse sways the ice inside his drink and searches his mind.

* * * *

She can see her knees in the mirror at the end of the room. Knobby, she thinks. I have these knobby knees, she thinks. She hides her boredom and she drinks her drink and Jesse speaks.

Sometimes I can't do it, he says. I really can't do it.

She nods and almost hums along with him while he's talking. Her eyelids slowly close as if not to miss a single word he's saying and she leans her head on the wall. Feeling the cocaine drips from the roof of her mouth she listens and watches him already remembering this exact moment. He moves his hands when he talks. His face disappears and his eyes glaze when he talks about the past and it's apparent on his face he is traveling back in time from one memory to the next.

* * * *

The thing is.
I don't know how to be good anymore, he says.
The thing is.
I can't find anyone, he says.
She doesn't know why while listening to him, she wants her hair pulled by him.

* * * *

He says, When I was younger, there was this girl on my street who followed me to school. A girl in a hoodie. The middle school was only few blocks away from where I lived and I lived right next to this girl. We were neighbors. We left home together at the same time in the morning and would point at each other sometimes without saying anything. Some days she did not acknowledge me at all and walked ahead of me.

One day she stopped a few paces ahead of me. She stopped in my favorite spot along the fence on the way to school. I could see her up ahead waiting for me. It was the only spot on the fence with vines and thorns and small dead flowers. I remembered thinking I liked the way the metal from the fence twisted into the flowers and I liked the smell. There was always loose trash around. She waited there for me. It felt to me like an adult moment.

I am thirteen.

Do you want to walk with me? She says to me.

We were neighbors and the same age. There was no avoiding one another. We went to the same school. Our mornings were the same mornings. I heard yelling coming from her house when there wasn't much yelling coming from my house. Before talking and getting to know her, I wondered how she dealt with being sad and quiet. I wondered how smart she was because I knew she was a genius.

She had a way of making our walks pleasant. She asked me about my life and the televisions shows we liked.

She was scary because she was young. She asked me about my mother and how I felt about death. We talked about Ren and Stimpy and books and rock music.

I thought, Who the fuck was this girl? Where did she come from? She was so intimate and forward and completely surprising, it made me imagine a good life. I started to see myself in the future surviving harder scenarios. I was getting beaten down by other men. I was in a small car accident. I could see myself near death and still wanting to be alive. There were scenes in my imagination where it's just us holding each other overlooking the neighborhood.

She was so intimate to me so quickly, she felt like a time traveler or something. Like she was my protector. Sometimes we would ditch class together, you know? And find a place to hide and mess around.

*   *   *   *

Around the same time my mother was having an affair. Jesse takes a sip from his whiskey as though the whiskey was water. He says, And she was not discreet. My mother was not discreet.

She often spoke to her new boyfriend on the speakerphone in the house when my dad wasn't home, Jesse says. I don't know why she always used the speakerphone. Her children could hear everything. I remember studying her and her conversations like a movie like I was already detached from everything.

Jesse takes another drink and stops talking.

He stares at the girl laying on the bed of the motel room that they paid for together. She is still wearing her high heels.

She says, Hi, Person.

He says, Hi, Person.

He says, You're still wearing high heels.

She says nothing.

* * * *

Have you ever done anal? Jesse asks her.

Yes, she says. I love anal.

She pauses and says, There is something perfectly wrong about it. I tend to love things I'm not supposed to love.

She says, Yes, I love anal. It feels wrong and good.

She finishes the contents of her drink and sucks on little pieces of ice. She asks, Why do you ask?

Jesse says nothing. He asks, Why do you ask?

Jesse raises his glass as though saying cheers with his eyes on her.

He says, We lose our virginity. She was my first time. We were happy and tried a lot of things. Our first time was in a car in a parking lot. There was desert and houses on both sides of us in the parking lot. For some reason we wanted it that way, especially after it was over.

* * * *

We tried anal like a week after that, Jesse says. Jesse turns on and off the radio with a remote control. The button lights on the remote control illuminate the dim room.

He says, It was after we saw a movie from the old one-screen movie theatre. We watched a movie starring James Spader and car accidents.

We thought we belonged in a movie. Running to the car at the end of the parking lot, she was already unbuttoning things like her shirt and pacing her breath. It was that excited kind of laughing that comes before touching. Her jeans were already on the dashboard and the heaters were turned on. There was cold breeze all around the car.

She was laying down reclined on the passenger seats. She was laying down on her stomach.

She said, I'm laying on my stomach, Jesse.

She said, Try something new.

Jesse says, My expression fell apart in a second. I was very charmed and mesmerized by her and I could feel the wanting leaving my face.

She readied herself by breathing slowly and smiling optimistically.

* * * *

Laying down on the bed, listening to Jesse, she realizes she is an unnamed girl. She realizes how high and warm she feels. She finishes another drink and feels deep in the blankets. His vulnerability is attractive and worth her time, she thinks.

They meet at her local dive bar and when she makes eyes with him, sticking their tongues at each other. Slender in her black dress, she sticks her tongue out to Jesse, which he can see through the silhouettes of people shooting pool, people getting more drinks, heading to restrooms. She unveils her back muscles when she takes off her jacket. For twenty minutes or so, they exchange eye contact with their tongues stuck out at a dive bar.

She exits when he exits and they talk outside.

* * * *

The same song plays again, *Lover's Spit*. She makes a deci-
sion. She could go for hours and hours in this fantasy.

She asks, What happened to her? What was her name?

Wendy, he says. He hands her a new drink.

My father found out about my mother's affair and
we had to leave the state, he says without expression. Jesse
does not move.

He says, It was a rough divorce. After I left, Wendy
and I lost touch almost immediately.

Yes?

Yes.

They listen to the cooling vents and the water pipes.
She thinks the DJ of the radio show must be asleep or
away from the keyboard or something. They keep playing
the same song over and over again without commercials.
The time on the radio face is a quarter past three in the
morning.

She says, Come on. She takes his wrist to the middle
of the room next to the television. They slow dance in
the middle in the room reflected on the television. He
trembles a little and she does not tremble at all.

Did you ever go looking for her, she asks?

Yeah.

Oh yeah?

Yeah. Once. He says. I came back to the city. But I
couldn't remember what her face looked like.

She takes his hand and places her head on his collarbone. Jesse holds her.

Do you know this song? She asks.

No.

No? Don't you know it by now? They've been repeating this song the whole night.

He says, Yes, actually.

They move as though attached. They slow dance alone in the motel room and she normally doesn't have these kinds of nights or say yes to strangers but she remembers approaching him thinking, You look like someone I already know. She remembers he looked fucked up too. Her hair's a mess. His face unshaven.

She says, what if I am Wendy?

Jesse says nothing.

She says. I'm serious.

She said, Try something new.

nights and weekends

I have dreams where I am Elliott Smith and I stay all day in coffee shops, writing songs with a black pen in my spiral ring notebook. The place is crowded and people move in slow waves edging themselves near the front where I am waiting. Everyone looks beautiful tonight. In my dream body, I have deep holes in my chest I am over six feet tall I have long brown hair and no one here can ask me my name. They know my name is Elliott Smith. I can sing the saddest songs in the world. Everyone in the crowd is another face. For waves and waves of people, there are more faces under the light, coming and going from various exits.

The day later feels bovine and softly restless. I order Vietnamese coffee with a single shot of espresso and wait there while staring at clouds. My body feels at rest underneath large tree branches in the shade. There are dozens and dozens of strangers here. No one yet has broken the ice or taken hands or embraced. The girl at the coffee cart leans and yells out, Single Vietnamese, and I reply, Yes I am and I smile like nobody's business.

I imagine a world where sadness has become illegal and I think this place will be named America. The new flag is a giant waving smiling happy face and I feel so demented when I see it. Crying will be something people do in secret, in cars parking lots and basements, as though it was a recreational drug to pass and share back and forth, better than alcohol. Every home town seems to have the perfect view at a high place.

She is more or less facing me. She is Mary in all of my stories. Mary is a girl from the future: someone who I think will keep talking to me all the way into the future, placing me somewhere dear in her memory.

She says, Beauty is in the eye of the beholder and what I need now is a beholder. We listen to Elliott Smith songs on the floor and discuss his death and open a bottle of champagne in order to get closer to each other. She says, In my room we are taking drugs together in my room.

We have filmed our entire lives and played the unedited coverage on the walls from a projector for anyone to see, for everyone to see. Some days other than two blank faces nothing new plays on the white sheets on the walls. There are days and days of footage when neither of us are on screen because we are looking at each other's screen. She waits to feel a thrill however distant.

I come home, exhausted one day, needing to talk to her. The key takes a little while to turn, to open the door. The television is on mute and the dishes are clean in the rack. She sits there stirring her tea, more or less facing me.

Mary is stoned, still sitting on the couch in the living room, half naked in her panties. She tells me, I'm really into stirring right now.

sky up

Some parties are forgettable, Alyssa says, how many parties have we had this week? She turns on the bath-room faucet but does not wash her hands or look down, staring at herself casually in the mirror, listening to the water. Her big lips crack as they smile. Alyssa feels the edge of the sharp blade of her pocket knife with her thumb, and winces just before it breaks the skin, before she hears a knock on the door. If you've been through hell, keep going, she says. She walks outside still holding the knife. She walks a straight line in one direction, because one direction is consoling, softening her focus, rubbing the bridge of her nose with her other hand before descending downstairs. The person in the front of the line, waiting for the bathroom, a girl wearing a bikini, says, Winston Churchill. The girl in a bikini says, That girl walking away holding the knife is quoting Winston Churchill.

Everyone is staring at Alyssa as she is walking to the kitchen, almost tripping and falling, still visible to everyone upstairs. Alyssa says, I keep going. Her face looks peaceful but distracted. Almost immediately, she throws the pocket knife in the sink, and grabs another drink from the mini-bar. Oscillating fans blow in her face and hair, cool her skin. Dipping her hands into the ice cooler, she takes a shot of whiskey before grabbing a beer. Usually drinking too much makes her stomach ache, but right now she is making an exception: she has seen some unbelievable things, sucking the blood from the small cut from her thumb.

Chloe is rubbing an ice cube against Alyssa's neck, suddenly appearing from behind her in the kitchen. Alyssa barely trembles. Chloe says, The people upstairs are all chanting Winston Churchill, I don't know why. Alyssa and Chloe exchange silent, shocked glances at each other for fun, something they do sometimes in spite of each other, for force of habit. Sitting together on the last step of the soft carpeted stairwell, they share the beer in tiny gulps, in shocked glances. They ask each other at the exact same time, both smiling, Guess what?

Alyssa says, I am not going to kill myself anymore.

Chloe says, I think I want to quit my job.

* * * *

JESSE

I can be someone who, all the time, ignores omens. I have seen things I would not know how to explain in the least bit. A girl offers her bare stomach for the lines of cocaine and pulls up her shirt. She swallows vodka like water and unhooks her bra. I watch a reflection of the ceiling fan on the glass coffee table before she lays down. Another girl leans down and kisses her bellybutton, taking a line. Feeling strangely calm, I don't join the cheering that happens around us, or the tensed hurried way everyone is scooting closer. The girl laying down says, Everything in modera-tion. Although this is my house, this is my party -- we are all sitting together in my guest room and there are burning candles on the carpet -- I don't know anyone intimately in the circle. Everyone here is a stranger.

Someone jumps from upstairs, a girl in a small bathing suit, right into the hardwood floors. She falls so hard she dislocates her shoulder, gasping and out of breath. Getting up, she pops her shoulder right back into place and waves to Alyssa. The girl says, Winston Churchill.

Once I tried to kill myself in front of my webcam to preserve the moment; I broadcasted trying to hang myself live on the Internet. The feed went viral in less than an hour, in about a dozen countries, in four different time zones. When I was still breathing through my nostrils, more and more people logged on and watched me swinging. I woke up dehydrated and Internet famous, and then police and paramedics arrived at my door in the morning. I remember saying, I lived, I lived, as an answer to every question that came to me. I wanted to announce tonight that I made a mistake, and feel so happy to be alive, but I haven't found the right moment to speak. I have been lingering and locked in for the past few hours, unsure of myself.

Chloe walks over to the ice cooler and grabs another drink, before smiling brushing past me. I try and mimic her face, and our two smiles grow larger when there is eye contact. I wonder how far our party can be heard in the neighborhood and turn to look out the porch. I can see dozens of open lit windows and people framed inside their houses.

She says, I've seen your video. She says, I've sought you out. I am falling in love with this Internet thing.

She looks at me in a way that causes me to blink first, before Alyssa comes to join us from the kitchen, wrapping her arms around me. Alyssa says, There was a girl that dislocated her shoulder. I look at Chloe before answering, I think I saw everything from here. Both girls are biting their lips and I am wearing down. Chloe mumbles, Maybe we should kick everyone out and just be here by ourselves, just us three. It is as though I had forgotten how to nod when I finally do, when Alyssa squeezes tighter, when Chloe keeps looking at me, the entire house still vibrating with music and strangers, and I keep nodding.

old tampons

Long distance relationships are like believing in God and do you want to believe in God again?

From the corner of the room I can see the mummy of an old tampon, the last thing she leaves me before departing back to Boston and there is a slow sunrise outside the bedroom. I live like my West Coast, blue and large and dangerous. The water shimmers with ships and boats on the shoreline.

Jane leaves my house wearing her skinny black dress before her chocolate cookies are finished baking, and burning and crumbling inside my shitty oven. I like her short black dresses and the way she is hurting because she has to leave me. I am thinking, when she turns back around to look at me in a slight moment before the door, if the look on her face had a caption, if her facial expression were to be translated to words, they would be *goodbye* and *Jesus* and *please call me*. They would be, *Please call me when my plane lands.*

I tell her on a note she finds later in her jacket pocket at the airport: *Fear expands me as well.*

She texts me about it and I don't answer my phone right away. For a few days I don't answer.

Glass balls are dropping everywhere in the cities of America. Skies are all on fire. Blue and orange and yellow.

Fireworks and new years. Crowds of warm people. All the stations broadcast celebrations.

Jane asks me, Would you like to watch television on the television?

I say, Of course. I would love to do that with you.

Much later in the evening when she says it, the word *Jesus* means complete pleasure and whole agony of the heart. The word *Christ* means Christ.

She takes off her dress and she pulls loose my belt. She has gotten used to me. She knows how to drink wine and how to drink wine and knows how to make a linguist useless. I can speak forty different languages and yet none when she plays her dance music.

Jane is on her plane and she is sadder and sadder. She is reading Milan Kundera. She is reading the line: *There is no balm more soothing for a man than when he knows he can cause sadness in a woman.* Flying over the ocean always makes her feel so low.

She writes in her notebook on the plane, *To fuck a God is how a person feels infinity. To love a person is how to feel finite again.* The wanting yearning feeling leaves her face when she goes for a walk to watch the cars pass by, when she gets back home to Boston. She has no idea what she is thinking. She tries to look at every driver in the face speeding by on the highway. She is twenty-nine in a long distance relationship.

After Jane is gone I have to clock into work at the Food Co-op and I am late again.

My friend Alyssa arrives to the Food Co-op and complains about her day while spinning in a mirror. She tells me she is gaining weight. I disagree with her right away.

What are you kidding? I tell her, I don't think so.

I say to her, I think that you're merely just appearing.
Turn around.

animals

vitamin d milk

Before anything else, he realizes he is a person. He has some-how reached this point in his success to consider the ques-tion of what is a good person? He is feeling quite detached from where he is. On TV the camera slowly zooms out and frames him in the scene. The stadium is a closed roof sta-dium and filled to capacity. There are no clear faces in the crowd that can be seen from the ring, only colors. Mouths open and close and form loud haunting chants. Flashing cameras illuminate small pockets of the crowd.

Everyone is having a profound moment of art.

The fighters are losing weight at every blow, as though evaporating. Red gloves glow like neon. The opponents circle and hover above the canvas.

He punches like he doesn't remember who he is and begins to drift elsewhere. He keeps breathing, letting in more pain. He is punching and blocking out the sound of the crowd.

A woman whispers to her husband in the crowd, God in heaven, he is going to kill him, and the husband wonders about the bet he's made. The crowd cheers and wants.

River punches relentlessly beyond thought.

The bell rings.

His eyes are cuts; buzzing lights hang above them like a floating city. There is a slight peace in standing still in the center of noise.

He knows to let it envelope him now.

He knows this strange peace when being very still when being watched or being filmed.

His face is the only clue people rely on. River wonders if Sam is watching the fight, if she is sitting down or walking around, if she is eating food or listening and glancing over at the television as she walks her dishes to the sink. His face is a question to the people jeering and the men commentating and the flashes competing for pictures and Sam is at home, watching his response.

good for you

Sam asks if he wants to swim, standing on the other side of the patio. The pool water jets therapeutically and softly in the underwater light. In the dark, River says nothing and begins undressing. They are left alone to do whatever they want in the winter, when the water is freezing cold, undisturbed by other tenants. No one else wants to swim in the pool but River and Sam in the winter. There is something revolutionary and nervy about swimming pools at night, he thinks. Dirty red leaves float on the dark slow moving surface. When he turns his head slightly back around, they consider each other. The pool is at the center of the apart-ment complex, with surrounding walls with closed blinds and windows, hanging laundry.

Sam comes closer and squeezes different parts of him and stays at his arm. He only acknowledges her by tensing his back muscles in her hands. She can hear the water lapping at the sides of the dark blue pool. Palm trees drag and sway framing the sky.

She looks at her hands on his back as though dreaming them there. But she moves her hand and the hands move.

River dives into the freezing pool under a breeze and splashes below. Under cold water, in slight agony and pleasure, he can hear muffled slow traffic from the road. His ears pop and pop. Touching the bottom of the pool, he stretches his back muscles and hamstrings and thinks he wants to die.

From above, Sam stares at the closed double doors from the wrought iron gated entrance before lowering herself to the floor with her chin on her knees. There are a few glow in the dark green signs that read NO HORSEPLAY. There are no traces of birds or small animals on the ground or in the dimly lit trees. Without moving a muscle, she is very close to the homeostasis state.

Laying down, she folds her hands on her stomach and watches a slow shooting star turn into a small plane into blue and red blinking lights.

River gets out of the water and drips footsteps around her. The body changes temperature around his lungs and face.

She says, When you went into the pool without me. You abandoned me in that moment.

She says, It was nasty of you.

She realizes her mind trying to shut River out for weeks now. When he comes up in conversation between friends or strangers, she abstains from saying anything. When talking, she has been enjoying just looking off in her hands. She remembers going to the grocery store earlier in the day, not wanting to buy anything for either of them. They both sink into the hot tub, the milky light, the rising steam.

He says nothing.

She asks, Yes?

He says, Yes.

I felt no obligation for some reason, to answer you.

                    *   *   *   *

He asks if he is striking a nerve, whether or not he is
upsetting her. She wants to tell him anecdotes and ignores
the question. Lately, they have been openly ignoring
each other's questions. Often instead they only exchange
stories with things they see throughout the day, of
common people and familiar faces they see everyday. Sam
cups the water jet with her palm. She has been having
uneventful dreams, like one where she is only looking to
answer a craving for Diet Coke. She is walking somewhere
imagined in a dream city or along a highway. She wakes
and sleeps next to him. The days suck into weeks into
months and assemble them-selves into the future.

He says, You never answered my question.

She says, Because it was a mean question. You know
what you're doing.

River says, This feels like an energy ball. My hand on
the water jet.

She says, I was just thinking that, staring at the jet on
her side of the pool.

He says, You were just thinking that.

good for you, honey

In the kitchen, they frost a cake together without special occasion. She says she thought of him earlier today going to the grocery store. She says after the errand, she went for a walk and watched cars pass by, turning the wide curve under willow trees next to the apartment complex. She feels every car pass, not hitting her, and she archives her feelings. For days, unsaid things are more and more common occurrences between them, like once in the morning in the mirror in the bathroom, when they catch eyes brushing their teeth and distance themselves. They have matching towels they regret buying. She wonders if there is something wrong with him.

He says, Fuck, and stubs his toes everywhere in the apartment.

She begins movies on demand without him. She becomes someone whose personal trivia has changed, replacing her old favorite movies with new favorite movies. Some days, he stands there from behind the couch watching her silently as though just accessing memory.

On the dining room table, there are two unopened cardboard boxes of creative wedding invitations, those with fine ink lace and paper, and early wedding presents. For a week, they eat frozen fruit smoothies from a brand new blender, and discuss breaking up. River watches a space on the couch beside Sam and contemplates sitting down before sitting down, and he brings her a drink. They have received three of the exact same blenders new knives and various designer picture frames. The tension between them can still sometimes lead to sex and brief moments of wanting each other. They pull hair and remain quiet, not speaking.

He calls from the grocery store and ask if they need any more strawberries or anything else.

She says, I am watching a movie, not answering the question.

River says, Bitch.

She asks, What are you saying? Are you calling me a Bitch?

He says, You don't remember. It's from a movie we watched together. A man says Bitch to his wife while he is being wheeled away on a stretcher or something to an ambulance and she thinks he is calling her a Bitch. But he was just quoting a movie they watched before.

Sam says, I don't remember.

She says, I think we're low on milk and cantaloupe too.

He says, Fucking Bitch.

She says, Fucking Asshole.

River says, Right now, I am riding the shopping cart. up and down and back and forth the aisles, and everyone is looking at me. All the employees.

He listens to her falling asleep on the phone, holding the phone with his shoulder, while he picks up two gallons of milk and a magazine for her to read, the special issue of Vanity Fair with her favorite Hollywood people on the cover. He sleeps with his arm around her while she doesn't move.

homogeneous

Sam leaves a room like someone who will be right back, and does not look back once she has started to leave even if it's before she knows where she is going. After their most recent argument, one ending with throwing furniture and shoes not at each other but at the walls and down staircases, Sam feels vague and foreign to the apartment that used to be their apartment. The television illuminates the dark warm living room while the microwave illuminates the small narrow kitchen. Sam spins around, contemplating her relationship, where her home is. She cannot tell what, inside her, is innate. The lining of her stomach hums and grows tense. She eats black ice cream and quivers as River is driving to the coliseum. Even when very tired, she can watch television for hours and feel close to bliss. Absolute bliss. She belongs to a particular space on the carpet, a certain cushion on the sofa, the middle of her bathtub, and the space between her bed and wall.

There are times she wants to be unbearable. For an instant, she feels as if she and River have been carrying on some other conversation, role playing the lives of some other couple this whole time. Perhaps they have not been fighting for weeks. Perhaps this all has been just one of them imagining things. She has been asking herself questions in the presence of friends and inanimate objects. Most days, she feels better just walking outside, walking for hours, in stupid directions and small circles around the block.

On the television: River is fighting his match. River seems to be doing okay, although she cannot tell. He has not been hit in the face for quite some time. When watching his matches, she cannot help looking away during the surreal moments. River sometimes mouths her name.

Only in these moments he calls her Samantha.

She keeps the television on when she leaves. On the screen, River's laughter has been going on for some time, through multiple rounds, catching the attention of other channels, broadcast stations, gossip networks. His laughter, his laughing, has been aired as a heartbreaking, strange coming of age story of a young champion, as though they have been there all along. The whole world has been right there all along.

Sam calls Mary.

Mary asks, Why is he laughing? I don't get it.

Sam says, Can you come and pick me up? I am already. walking toward you.

try me

Everyone at the party is sadly talkative. Sam wonders how long her shoulders have been shaking, leaning against the wall, overlooking the scene. She has been clumsy. She has small bruises on her face and arms from hitting the car door on the way here when first arriving to the party: the house with the lush green lawn. She has small bruises from a lot of things. Walking across the main floor, Mary hands her a cold beer touches her shoulders and says, I can't leave you alone for a minute. Mary smacks Sam's face with a red slab of meat inside a plastic bag.

She says, For the face.

Sam holds the plastic bag and then lets it slip from her hand, dropping to the carpet.

Sam says, Fuck steak.

She says, Fuck my life. Fuck steak.

Mary says, Language, language.

Mary says, You should pretend you're someone else for the night.

Sam says nothing but watches.

Mary says, I mean, I do that from time to time. I pretend to be someone else. She finishes the contents of her drink, tilts her head back, and smiles to Samantha before she asks, Does anyone call you Samantha anymore?

Sam wonders if her face will explode and caresses the

bruises on her face. She feels warm. The party is themed THE END OF THE WORLD PARTY, although there are no banners or anything. She arrives feeling unprepared slender and out of place. She wonders what she should have worn for the end of the world. She asks, Whose house is this?

Mary says, you know this house. She says, this is Rich-ard's house.

Mary gets the meat from the plastic bag on the carpet. She throws it against a glass sliding door and laughs at the impact.

try me

He looks a little white, standing there by the oven. Richard can spot Mary in a crowd almost immediately. There is something about the way they recognize each other: a strange skin deep chemistry as comfortable as can be as though the room is shrinking them closer together.

There is something about winter nights. She has developed, over the years, a habit of tucking her hair behind her ears when she does not want to cry. It is neither a nervous gesture or a bad sign. She is prophetic. Richard walks sideways and moves in between people talking in the crowd. Sam watches him cross the kitchen holding a bottle of wine in his hands above his head, already remembering it, mak-ing him her most recent memory.

He asks Sam, Have you been watching the fight?Sam says nothing.

He asks, Do you want to drink this together and watch the fight? I have a radio.

Wouldn't we be listening then, Sam asks. Rather than watching?

He says, I have a television.

Mary massages Sam's back muscles from behind and says, That sounds nice. Let's all watch the fight together.

There's a room upstairs at the end of the hallway. They walk upstairs and watch the party unveil from room to room and door to door, having brief snapshots of people touching: hardcore hip hop in one room, people kissing in one closet, a man and a woman in bathing suits and a ukulele on the floor with the door ajar. Sam walks barefoot. Everyone slowly dips their head back and registers pleasure, spacing off, eyes glaze. They grieve in another world for this one.

Richard, Mary, and Sam lay on the floor and stay like that listening to the radio while watching the television, sharing bottles of wine and champagne. The night air is becoming lighter and thinner.

Sam is the first of any of them to be looking torn, her head swimming in the stillness of the room. She listens to flowing water in some pipe somewhere in the house, some pipe she cannot see.

* * * *

Sam feels a scraping sensation in the back of her throat. Sam reaches over to touch Mary's hand, who touches Richard's hand, who touches Sam's. He says, Maybe we need to get up. Mary says, I remember how we all used to lay around like this. In the summer. Sam brings her face closer to Mary's neck and collarbone and lies there, pulling along Mary's blouse unconsciously, exposing her navel and small stomach, wrapping her arms around Mary. Sam listens to the crowd cheering on the television which gives the room it's only light, her mouth open. The walls change color depending on what happens elsewhere. On the television, River wipes his mouth on the back of his hand and Richard and Mary and Sam try it out too tangled together on the floor.

Downstairs there is still the party. People in little groups in corners. Sometimes there are quiet moments when no one has anything to say, cosmically timed with when the song changes.

She is one to get excited when no one else in the room is talking. Being quiet, Sam has learned, is a ceremonious way to communicate, an undisclosed way to touch someone. The eyes can be a vacation for someone looking. She feels sorry for all the people who don't realize their world could change in a second. She imagines the last time she made love to River, only a few days ago, and resists the temptation to break her eye contact with Mary. She imagines the last time she made love to Mary and Richard. She thinks, They could waste their entire lives talking.

Richard leaves the room and climbs down the stairs,

heading to the stereo. The power fluctuates in the house, the lights get dim. He tells everyone he has called the police. Please leave. Richard flickers the lights on and off.

Mary kisses Sam on the forehead, on her eyebrow.

She says, Please don't kill yourself.

Sam says, I am not going to kill myself.

* * * *

On the television, a young man named Thom wins an Olympic gold medal in high diving without knowing how to swim. There is slow motion footage of him diving beautifully cutting clean into the pool. Underwater, Thom faints and floats suspended with his arms and legs hanging out, his hair continuing to wave, waiting for scuba divers to come and retrieve him.

The pool appears deep and tranquil, appearing undisturbed by his presence. Men drag him from the edge of the pool carefully. When he wakes up, everyone is standing and applauding, including the announcers, other divers, and the cameramen. He waves to the crowd laying on his back, just now regaining consciousness, and then he waves some more with two hands. He makes a calm facial expression, as though casually waking up in bed. This is how he always dives.

River wins his match. The past twenty minutes have been shots of the crowded ring, tracking paramedics and River being padded onto a stretcher with a bloody mouth. River is smiling with a bloody mouth, spitting away a microphone. The words are captioned on screen in white letters. In his short sound bite, when asked how he is doing, River says, I want to be unbearable.

He says, I formally retire from the world of professional boxing. A close up. Then commercials.

Richard walks back into the room shutting the door closed behind him. Everyone has left the party, leaving the house empty feeling as though it's a brand new space. The windows and blinds are open. He has a series of days, of rough weeks in his life, he could forget entirely. He has a ukulele in his hand. Richard says, I found this, in the next room, near some bathing suits.

Mary strips and walks barefoot around the house, moving her body from room to room, sometimes running or jogging. She is closing all the blinds and windows, but turning on most of the lights and ceiling fans. She remembers there is nothing like really being held, arrested under bright lights or in the dark, really being held close to someone. Finally, Mary sprays perfume in the bathroom and walks through the cloud, turning on the stereo with a remote control from the doorway. She tiptoes on hardwood floors.

The stereo face reads GUIDED BY VOICES—BLIMPS GO 90.

Mary asks, Is everyone gone?

Richard says, Yes. Everyone is gone.

He plays ukulele and lays on the floor.

Sam puts a hand on her forehead and listens to noises in the air, laying flat in the doorway, half in the room. She can see what happens downstairs and watches Mary run around. Whiskey harms the way she lays there, almost outlining her body with warmth.

Richard asks, How did you get those bruises on your face?

She says, I fell on the way here.

He says, I don't think I believe that.

Mary struggles back into her clothes and waits for Sam in the kitchen, breathing cold air from the open windows. It's early morning. She ponders the chandelier and wants cocaine or a cold glass of wine. She says, There are things I could just never say to anyone. She walks into daylight, unaware of herself, with great posture and surrender. She is smoothing out the wrinkles of her denim tight jeans with her left leg, having not blinked for several minutes, appearing emotionless or transported; she is balanced there in the doorway. For a moment, in the mirror near the wooden coat rack, she is in love with her slightest bit of flesh caught between strap and armpit. The chandelier swings and makes shadows back and forth on the walls.

Upstairs, Richard is behind Sam, talking to Sam. The light in the room would make it good for taking photos, she thinks briefly.

He says, I stopped really caring about Mary when she started playing guitar, but that had nothing to do with it. I don't believe she wanted me anymore.

Sam says, I don't want River anymore. When I watch his boxing, I think about leaving him.

Richard says, Mary made me CDs I never listened to. Just recently, I started to make a stack of them next to my bed, so I wake up to them every morning.

Sam says, I do that.

He asks, You do that, Sam?

Sam says, I do that.

Mary gets into her car and looks for a cigarette. She forgets all about the cigarette when a song starts playing on the radio, and she realizes she has not heard this song in years. Something inside wins. She has an unopened pack of her favorite cigarettes hidden beneath her car seat.

Richard is looking at Sam.

Sam is looking at Richard.

She says, I don't know. I don't know. I think I just wanted everyone to be happy.

Leslie Cheung jumps off my building closes his eyes and then sings a song we both know and love

You leave the room and take the coffee pot with you to strange places in the house. I can imagine you with expressive faces holding coffee in the basement or the garage in the dark or outside near our tree. Sometimes, you say you don't like me. I can imagine every single outfit you have ever worn.

The tragic scene in the movie in which love dies or hope dies hardly moves us or causes any sensation in our bodies. A good cry has not happened in years. I am wearing the same things over and over again. Together we drink Diet Coke spiked with good whiskey. It appears I am focused on you. Diffused light milks our view from the bulbs with soft colors. You say I say the word milk too much. We pass hot popcorn with our hands. We are watching a movie we rented down the street a dozen times. There is moonlight on your face from the window. Even though we are angry we contemplate each other's mouths holding our ground and principles. Love feels like a thing people eventually learn to live without like tonsils or god.

* * * *

You have a dream about this. For the end of the world, everyone is having an end of the world party. Everyone we know is at this party. A friend of yours brings a megaphone to the party and intimately shares their secrets with everyone. Voices are snowy and garbled with static. Alone with your glass in the corner, you look out and feel the scene to be surreal. You even move your hands forward in front of you and clench your fists. You notice colors and old memories. You say, I can read your mind. You ask, If you can read mine is it yours. I watch you drink and wonder when you will become dangerous. When I drink red wine I know I will start mumbling eventually. You focus at squeezing the air at the bottom of your lungs, looking angry, walking past me three times. I follow you for a dozen laps around the kitchen, trying to hand you bread. Everyone else in the world is quiet in the living room in the dream. Your mother says she really likes me. Your boyfriend from the seventh grade is still a real asshole. I'm looking at him right now.

*　*　*　*

I am distracted by a phone call for weeks. I think maybe the world has really ended but apathy is more powerful. Do you remember how broadcast news used make us cry. Do you remember writing a note down to remind your future self to love the future. The feeling collects and collects inside everyone. I have a craving. I make the mistake looking up at our waitress last night while she was looking at you. She is not going to remember us. She comes up to us with more breakfast food and coffee. The steam from the plates makes the moment seamless. For some reason I remember you even calmer than you are. I am trying to tell you Leslie Cheung died almost ten years ago. We only have to wait a year or so to celebrate and rent *Happy Together* again. Yes, this entire time I have had some of your dress in my mouth. What is your problem.

planet b boy

Maybe a dozen red ambulances are passing outside the grocery store, all heading in one direction down the hill. There are calming bright lights in a row in the freezer aisle. Later he feels a dumb calming bliss from slipping the same type of milk into the same place in the refrigerator door taking longer than he should in the ongoing recycled air. He has a soft moment feeling alive staring at produce and boiled eggs. If he lays down here on the kitchen floor with the refrigerator open, if he can allow his mind to listen only to sounds of the cooling ventilation, isolating them to meditate and even out, will he be able to find his mind again?

He feels the efficiency of laying down without any thought. His face is against the cold tile.

B Boy Darkness says, I am sinking.

I am sinking because I am happy.

He extends his hands and meditates. His body is a star. He weighs less than a pound on the plain tile. The room turns blue when the sun sets and a strange unknown sound like a growl perhaps from the pipes vibrates the ground. For a moment he falls asleep.

* * * *

There is an unknown disaster happening down the hill. Small great fires. All the cars drive in unison with red ambulances together the highways away from the cities. She sees people collapsing in clumps down the hill on the streets. B Boy Darkness feels a scream as though it were coming from his own throat coming from someone down the hill. A few people are screaming at arguably the same thing. They are all feeling arguably the same thing. He stands next to the girl on the train, together with her looking at noth-ing but city lights. They are holding hands. Each finger has an independent tremble and coercion. He says, I am going to see what's happening. He says, I can dance so symmetrically for so long it can feel like nothing is happening. I can make my body a catastrophe.

*　*　*　*

He sees her every day when he rides the trains to practice. She tells him she admires him in a low dress. In his head, there are only a few things worth living for. He can no longer describe why the weight of his gym bag on his shoulder makes him feel intimate and tapped into the world. He explains to her, My hands are calloused from routine. He says, There is something peaceful about routine and let-ting go over what comes back to you. When the train car slowly brakes, and the automated female voice bleeds over the intercom from passenger car to passenger car, he feels unbridled glee when she comes a little closer to him. She moves away from the horror she sees down the hill from the window, where the people are screaming or afraid of death and she says, I was scared but now I'm better. I was scared before but now I'm better.

*   *   *   *

The mess she leaves is all in his head. She is amassing, still waiting on the train car in her own afterglow where he just left her, right next to the automatic sliding doors. She is holding the plastic railing with her might. Her body is getting smaller and smaller in the distance while he paces his breath and heads down the hill. B Boy Darkness is running down the hill in the middle of the street since no traffic is coming even through the tunnels. He runs until he gets there.

* * * *

Sometimes the crowds share one mesmerized face during a B Boy show. He has danced every day for the past few years with a signature presence. All the muscles in his arms glow in open tension. It's as if his body grows heavier after a performance when he is being watched but lighter when he is touched.

It will dawn on him to stop talking about love over and over again and rather just sit across the table from her in silence or stand closely next to her for a minute. He feels both. His face is still when he imagines the future with her the girl from the train car, staring out the window down the hill.

* * * *

Right away he starts breakdancing in his running shoes. There are some people lying on the pavement unconscious in the light. A fire hydrant is one giant geyser of water. He finds his center of gravity and starts to spin around and around again on his palms. While more red ambulances continue to arrive, and heat shimmers in the air in ribbons with black smoke and nearly blinds visibility, the scene inside the noise is calm and simple: Everyone is watching B Boy Darkness breakdance in the street, clumped in dozens down the hill, unable to describe how they feel, but they are all here together. They are dozens and hundreds feeling finally emotional. Every window in the buildings all around them has a face.

savannah

She spreads the legs of her tripod and barefoots back and forth from viewfinder to blankets on the floor. In her background long blinds swing in sunlight creating a warm cadence. Every time she peers through the hole she tip-toes without ever touching the camera with her face. She tells me I am her pear and wonders if she means pair. On speakerphone I am driving a fast car on the sidewalk trying to get to her. She narrates a different scene for me. If I was the phone, she says, I would be inside her pocket. She tells me she is doing laundry. She says, I am taking pictures of nothing again. I hear her occupying a body. She admits she was never really doing laundry.

* * * *

At parties no one parties. Events are not eventful. I go all day without talking to anyone. On the radio the DJs play faint new NO WAVE songs and refrain from talking into the microphone. Nights are hot enough for everyone to take off their sweaters and feel unwatched. She cleans her face in the sink and splashes cold water. She makes every outfit look so comfortable. She says, I'm afraid so, to someone calling her on her cell phone. Holding my hand in the hallway between our bathroom and our kitchen, she squeezes my hand in a way that imprints in my memory.

She looks through walls and door handles with a blank face in this way that reminds me it was hard for her to have it easy growing up. I never feel poor or lacking around her.

She looks at her hand between herself and the mirror. I know she tries to focus on where her hand is and not why she is still standing in front of the mirror.

In the shower her soft shapes belong to me. Our faces sometimes do not move. Some days I pan out my mind like a camera. Her eyelashes are longer than I remember her eyelashes being. In my head I reenact and cross out memories.

I am talking to my friend about his black argyle socks and how much I like them. Empty bottles of wine and tortilla chip crumbs already seed the floor. Our friends are all asleep in a clean living room huddled together. My head feels twice its size nestled against her on a couch. She asks me, How did we get to this party. I say, I don't know we were fighting the whole time.

*　*　*　*

She calls home with threats sometimes when she forgets herself. She chooses words like knife and love and I don't know if I can do this anymore. My friends call this a warning sign. If I don't catch myself, I can get angry at strangers and bus drivers when I arrive home late to see her. Sometimes a person to blame is the only faith I need. When she starts to throw steel toe shoes at my head, I am frightened with my polite tone of voice and the way she says my name. She says my name perfectly like I have been saying it wrong this whole time. I am giving her every priority.

One day on the bus I forgot which direction I was going. I say it out loud a few times. I say I forgot which way I was going.

* * * *

I go almost all year without laughing.

Chloe in the afternoon

The acceleration driving fast pulls her head back against the seat; the cool breeze from the open passenger window nearly blows her eyelids closed. Within view of the ocean, Chloe drifts from block to block until getting to the highway, the same cold morning over and over and over again, she thinks. She can do this every day. Before the highway, Chloe turns on the radio, shifts aggressively, and watches tree branches whip violently above the traffic lights. She can always imagine the end of the world at any idle moment, feeling the wind push and envelope her car. She is waiting at a stop sign not paying any attention to the radio or passing cars, or to the cop standing out in the road, turning traffic away.

Although she feels rushed, Chloe is the first one to arrive to the office, the only car in the parking lot on the hill, and she stares at the clock on her dashboard. There is a sad part of her that is always mouthing lyrics, and she catches herself singing unconsciously in the rear view mirror. For the first time in her life, before turning off the ignition and getting out of her car, she waits for the pop song to finish on the radio. Chloe sinks into her declined chair, arms outstretched almost to the threshold of pain. She says, I feel something. What am I feeling?

I can see a little life in you today, he says. The older

security guard here can always talk to her and make eye contact. Without wanting to, Chloe says, I can see a little life in you, repeating him, still waiting for the elevator. So many elevators. He presses the lit button a few times, which she finds strangely soothing. Chloe doesn't know why she said what she said, although it felt natural. Instead of thinking about it, she breathes in deeply and pretends she can see him from the back of her head. She mouths, I can see a little life in you. Chloe steadies her face in the window, becoming brave and exhausted when the elevator opens.

At work, she writes and stares at the Internet for hours, sometimes purposely without blinking. Most often, tears well up in her eyelids but never come to the point of crying. There are days when she gets closer and closer to the threshold, but she has never come close to crying at work, which she considers to be amazing. It has been a long time since she has felt this close.

There is a bird trapped inside the office building. Slowly people have begun to take notice, pointing and making faces and small enthusiastic commotion. The songbird does not seem frightened, flying from computer to computer, a young female starling. She sings a song for them, for all the pale workers, landing at one moment on Chloe's keyboard. She behaves herself, almost holding her breath, feeling nothing pending in the world, nothing foreboding, looking convinced of something.

Chloe says, I really like this bird, leaning back in her chair, suddenly really tired yet happy, and her chest is warm. The warmth in a way takes over. Her computer screen turns black and she could see in the reflection all of her co-workers, dozens and dozens of blended faces, standing behind her, watching the bird and the back of her neck. She says, If I don't fuck someone tonight, I think I might go insane.

She stands up from her swivel chair and walks to her manager's office. He's eating a very large sandwich, still chewing when she floats in. She demands a raise. A fucking raise now or I walk, she says. A piece of salami drops from his mouth and slaps his desk with specks of mustard, yellow stars.

when she pets the back of my neck I can be an animal

She says, I looked alive, to me in the mirror slowly raising her arms and then allowing me to pull her shirt over her head. In the shower she thinks about unfinished business with a very serious face; she is conscious of the water flowing over her body and we take turns underneath the shower head. This is an awkward dance. I don't ever ask her if she wants to shower with me. But sometimes she surprises me unlocking the bathroom door and she sneaks in the tub with me without a word when I am already soapy and entranced. In the dark she finds a new and interesting swagger. She shudders adjusting to the then perfect water temperature. She drives me mad with decisions. Yet I really enjoy being bewildered with all of her decisions watching her now playing with soap along her curves. Her hair clings around her forehead. She contemplates my mouth then kisses me in the shower. She says, Sometimes I get a little flagrant. She says, Don't ever tell anyone.

We eat Mexican rice and beans and remember all the things we've ever said. Sometimes she is very upset with me. Sometimes we revisit the first day we met or became aware of the other, reliving the memory like a silent movie, us ourselves still acting in the same movie still going on, sometimes narrating out loud. These are funny scenes together. It's like we're performing for the other person because we might get bored again. She makes a popping sound with her mouth. She steals another scoop of rice from my plate and I realize we have changed so much. The way we talk now and apologize to each other resembles dancing. She squeezes her eyes shut. She says, It's so bright out. In the sunlight along the couch in the living room I watch her shut her eyes more.

Suddenly we know we will live for a long time and survive everything. This calm happens while watching tele-vision or listening to a record lying on the wooden floorboards with sweaters on. Usually one of us is aroused by the other at all times. Where we put our hands is a game we play unacknowledged but we know we know. She likes my hand anywhere on her leg especially inside her thigh. When she pets the back of my neck I can be an animal. She mentions her sister coming into town to visit. I ask her if she is tired and she says, No, not really. Shadows give the living room an aquarium feel from the walls. There is always something I forget I should be doing right about now I think I say out loud. She says, Check out how blue the sky is outside. She says, When I say blue you say sky. She says, Blue.

Mary passes me on the way to the garage in the hall-way. She looks at me sideways readjusting the bag on her back mentioning something again about her sister coming to visit. Getting into the car to go pick up her twin sister, she watches the garage door slowly open, she watches a few cars pass on the road before merging. Traffic passes in glimmers and sound tunnels. I can hear birds returning. Sometimes she looks out the window and thinks very negative thoughts about people; she says, No one really knows how to be happy or live. Things like sparrows tiny leaves and debris in the wind and couples walking on the sidewalk pass in and out of her line of vision while we remember our way to the airport. Heat ribbons move in the air off the pavement and white lines. Exiting off the highway, she makes a contemplative yet happy face, taking off her sunglasses. Her eyes turn hazel from hazel. She says she felt really safe earlier when our arms touched each other in public and we made eye contact standing next to a fat man in the elevator in the parking garage where we first met casually. For fun she drives backwards on the 405.

how to survive a
car accident

Say "yes" when James invites you to L.A. with him for a weekend. Ask what kind of people are going to be there. Walk with your hands in your pockets and realize that you don't know James very well. Feel a warm and mutual respect because you have read his poems in class before and liked the one about the boy who eats a mockingbird. Have conversations about life and death and joke about it. Ask how did that topic come up in the first place.

Meet Jenny in a vacant parking lot, still blue colored from morning light. Look at her in the eyes because she is important to you. Lay on the roof of the car waiting for James in front of his house. Listen to Wu-Tang Clan vibrate the metal of the roof you're laying on. Imagine sitting inside a plane when one flies overhead. You could hear the drug-induced non-anxiety coating James's voice when he wonders where his keys are.

Take the I - 5 North towards L.A. / San Bernardino. Sit shotgun and get assigned to be DJ. Listen to the calming clicks from your iPod. Take peppermint gum from Jenny. Acknowledge you have never done anything with these two friends before. Jenny appears glowing while driving. James in the backseat sinks into the cushion, closes his eyes.

Open and close windows. Talk about past

relationships and laugh in unison during sexual parts. Get distracted with other passengers on the highway. Imagine relationships with those that make eye contact with you. Try, and remember Mary in a positive way and cut wind with your hand through your open window.

Play Rilo Kiley. Light a cigarette to share with everyone else in the car. Take unconscious drags of smoke.

Slowly pass a sixteen wheeler semi truck on your right hand side. Listen to Skinny Love. Notice a car up ahead swerving into your lane. Watch the car swerve back quickly to its own lane. Exhale when Jenny reacts and turns the steering wheel closer towards you. Hold the armrest while your own car swerves out of control. Notice how calm your breath is. Let things happen. Swerve into the semi on your right. Crash with the momentum of the cabin and everything behind you. Close your eyes. Duck somehow. The roof above you caves down and down again. The noise is tremendous. Glass shatters and rains in small bits and pieces and falls on top of your and your friends' jeans.

Realize the car is stuck moving underneath the semi. Get dragged underneath while the semi is braking on the I - 5 North.

Lose your glasses. See blurry and near sighted. Leave the car through Jenny's driver's side door and keep walking away. Feel a strange urge to keep walking away. Resolve to baby steps. Jenny is ahead and James is behind you. Ask if everyone is okay with your mouth.

Hear your friends say your name a few times. Watch Jenny cover her own mouth. Experience your blood filming over your cheeks. They say you are the only one injured.

Lay on the hot pavement in front of the truck. Realize you are still chewing your gum, while cars are still passing by. When James starts asking you questions about Rilo Kiley, notice the softness in his voice and realize he is trying to keep you conscious. Chew the stale gum and answer all his questions. Talk about everything you know about Rilo Kiley. Cover your head with James's white dress shirt. Hear Jenny crying and gasping while she is standing above you with her cell phone. Understand you have a gash. Say something weird, like you are still chewing your gum.

Love your life. Think about fighting.

Say you are conscious when a man appears. Say "thank you" when the man identifies he is a doctor, someone who had pulled over, dressed in civilian clothes. Say your name is "Richard" and call him "Brian." Say you are conscious when there are paramedics. Say you feel no pain in your legs when they ask. Look up at moving clouds when they massage you into a neck brace. Say you are conscious. This is the first time you have been inside an ambulance, so remember everything. Love your life. Feel convinced you have no regrets. Feel the ambulance drive away and the road beneath your back.

Ask how everyone else is doing. Notice how all the paramedics look at you in this way while they apply tubes and pat you down. They all say good. Listen to them discuss how you might be in shock.

Wonder if there is an imaginary clock somewhere inside you ticking. Stare at the ceiling and listen to sirens. Imagine traffic around you opening up and clearing a path. Move your fingers, move your toes inside your shoes.

Arrive safely to the hospital. Know without knowing you are going to be okay. Watch the ceilings change as they guide you down hallways, double doors and elevators. Ask more people how their days are. See smiles and feel touched you have the power to surprise them. Hear more talks that you are in shock. Enter the emergency room become tired under the lights and feel less conscious. Everyone wants you to stay with them. Listen to a disembodied voice, from a doctor walking around with an IV tower, describe your body parts. Your head is a gash. Your stomach is soft and supple. Realize your clothes are being cut with scissors and stay still. Say your name is Richard. Ask where you are. Ask anything you want to say, say anything you want to say.

* * *

Receive visits from nurses and doctors. Slowly feel aches and strange pains in broad places in your body. Learn Nurse Renee has been tending to you even when you were unconscious. Feel empty without reason when Nurse Renee tells you everything is going to be okay. Feel alive when she stays there with you for hours on a fold up chair. Your family has been notified. On your head, there are nine staples and dried blood.

Experience bliss in isolating sounds and thoughts and moving your lips slightly. Say you feel good. Ask where your friends are.

Leave the emergency room like nothing happened. Feel the sensation of being filmed when hugging James and Jenny and your aunt who arrives from Newport Beach, who all have been waiting for you in the waiting room. Look everyone in the eyes. Notice there are no magazines. Say you are ready to go.

Suddenly turn around and watch Nurse Renee run through some double doors to hand you a slip of paper. She says, "You'll be needing this."

Read a prescription for Vicodin with her name and signature. Watch her shake your hand and wait a moment before she leaves. Eat dinner at a Pho restaurant with your friends and aunt in your hospital gown. Devour hot food and noodles. Talk all night and teach Jenny and James how to say "We almost died" in American Sign Language.

* * *

Meet Mary in a parking lot, some place random in Santa Monica, and cringe when you notice her new boyfriend. Feel like you should have died when Mary makes a few jokes about Post Traumatic Stress Disorder and caresses her new boyfriend near his thighs. Listen to The Mountain Goats and remember you authored this mixtape for Mary and watch the highway for hours. Enjoy affinity and human connection watching James sign "We almost died" with his hands in the backseat with you. Listen to Mary joke more.

He says, "We should have called someone else to pick us up from L.A."

Say everything is okay. Find bits of glass everywhere for days.

Get invited to a Halloween party. Go to the Halloween

party and shake hands with people you know and people you don't know. Say thank you when someone compliments you on your costume, on how how lifelike the wound appears. Say hello. Lip sync some songs you like from the party. Sing the chorus. Rap "Living life without fear. Twenty five carrots in my baby girl's ear." Rap "Birthdays were the worst days. Now we sip champagne when we're thirsty." Say nothing when everyone repeats "party and bullshit," while leaning against a wall.

Laugh only when something is funny. When something is funny, remember to look someone in the eye because you liked what they just said. You want them to know.

YOU PRIVATE PERSON

acknowledgements

Thank you to Jon Nix and With an X Books for believing in me and for giving my book new life. Jon, you are the King of Ohio and I am thrilled and honored to know you.

Thank you to Tori Huynh for the gorgeous book cover.

Thank you to the editors who previously published some of the stories and different sections of *You Private Person in SLAB, Metazen, unsure if i will allow for my beard to grow longer, Housefire, kill author, Mud Luscious Press, Pangur Ban Party, for every year, Universal Error, New Wave Vomit, Thought Catalog, Everyday Genius, elimae, Smalldoggies Magazine, Titular, Monkeybicycle, City Arts Magazine, Poor Claudia, Vol. 1 Brooklyn, and 3:AM Magazine.*

Thank you to others who unknowingly provided words and phrases and ideas for use in the writing of *You Private Person*: Masha Tupitsyn in *Beauty Talk & Monsters*; Danielle Dutton in *S P R A W L*; Blake Butler in *Ever*; Amina Cain in *I Go To Some Hollow*; Graham Foust in *As In Every Deafness*; Robert Lopez in *Part of the World*; Miranda Mellis in *The Revisionist*; the film *Half Nelson*; the film *Nights And Weekends*; the documentary *Planet B Boy*; David Simon in *The Wire*; Ellen Kennedy in *Sometimes My Heart Pushes My Ribs*; the band Rilo Kiley; the band Broken Social Scene; the band Guided By Voices; the band High Places; The National, Bright Eyes, Elliott Smith; St.Vincent; Sufjan Stevens; Tao Lin; Eileen Myles; Dennis Cooper.

Thank you to Blake Butler, Dennis Cooper, and Kate Zambreno for honoring my book in 2012 with their blurbs. I am eternally grateful.

Thank you to Spencer Madsen and Sorry House Classics.

Thank you to Jeremy Spencer and Scrambler Books.

Thank you to all my readers and thank you for championing my work.

EXIT

ABOUT THE AUTHOR

Richard Chiem is the author of *You Private Person* (With an X Books, 2024), and the novel, *King of Joy* (Soft Skull, 2019), which was long listed for the 2020 PEN Open Book Award. He was named a 2019 Writer to Watch by the *Los Angeles Times*. He was also a judge for the 2023 PEN/Robert J. Dau Short Story Prize for Emerging Writers. He lives in Seattle.

Author photo by Bella Petro Photography

WITH AN